Theater Voyeur
Book One: Lights

An Erotic Amsterdam Novella

By

Annelise Fox

First published in Great Britain in 2014
by LionheART Publishing House
www.lionheartgalleries.co.uk
publishing@lionheartgalleries.co.uk

Copyright ©2014 by Annelise Fox
ISBN: 978-1-910115-11-4

1

"Quick, up here!" Andreas grabs my hand and pulls me into a cobblestone alley off Nieuwmarkt.

He pushes me up against the brick wall of the brothel housing the three women we have just watched mutually masturbate in contravention of Amsterdam's surprising, and occasionally contradictory, sex laws.

Andreas pulls the neckline of my shirt down, popping the button, and feasts on my breast through my lace bra. I push my chest further into his face and he yanks my bra up before teasing my nipple with his teeth.

I moan and reach for his belt with shaking hands. We've been going through a tough time lately and it's been too long since we let ourselves go like this. I unbuckle, unbutton and unzip, then slip my hand through the very 'handy' slit in his boxers.

I pause as a group of drunken, horny men pass the entrance to the alley, no doubt having just been treated to the same show we have. One of them catcalls and I grin. They can't see our faces in the gloom, but we're close enough to the alley entrance that they won't mistake what we're doing.

"Are you okay, Liesel?" Andreas pauses and moves slightly to hide me from the men's stares.

I smile again and kiss him. I still have hold of his cock and slowly move my hand up and down his silky shaft. I can feel his smile in his kiss as he hungrily thrusts his tongue in my mouth and explores its recesses.

His cock hardens further and my fingers aren't long enough to completely encircle him. I thrust my hips towards him and feel Andreas place his hands on my skirt, then yank it up—to more catcalls and whistles from our audience.

I'm not wearing panties—a dare by Andreas—and I move my feet apart, desperately wanting him inside me. I have not been this excited for a long time.

Andreas thrusts his hips toward me and I let go of him to grasp his buttocks as the tip of his cock nudges my cleft.

I stand on tiptoes and spread my legs further apart, desperate for him.

But he's in playful mood: delaying, teasing, increasing the anticipation. He grabs my shirt and rips it open, burying his head in my breasts.

I fling my head back and yell in pain as it connects with the wall behind me.

"Go on, do her, mate, she's begging for it!" The men are British then, probably a stag party.

Andreas lifts his head to look at me in concern. "Well, go on, do as you're told," I say.

"You've had too much to drink."

"No—too much to smoke." I giggle. "You know how horny weed makes me!"

"You sure?" he asks, with a nod to the street. I look at the men. At least they're shielding us from the rest of the busy street. I notice one of them fondle himself through his jeans. Probably the groom—unless he's in the brothel.

I turn back to Andreas, dig my fingers into his ass and moan "Fuck me" into his mouth as I kiss him again.

He bends his knees and adjusts a little, finding my slit with his cock. He pushes and I moan, banging my head again, as he fills me.

We've been together two years, and our sex has gotten us through every problem we've encountered. He reaches parts of me no man has ever found before, and even now the sensations to which he subjects my body surprises me.

When he's fully enveloped, he pauses, then slowly withdraws.

"Ahhh," I groan.

"That's it, you go, girl!"

"Fuck me," I say again to Andreas, louder this time; loud enough for the men to hear. I glance over at them; they've moved closer, into the shadows, but not close enough to be a threat. Three of them have their dicks out and are masturbating. I grin. *How many men can I make come in the next few minutes?*

2

I turn my attention back to Andreas as he thrusts hard, and cry out as heat flashes through me. "Oh my God, yes," I pant, and Andreas pushes into me again and again.

I lift one leg and he knows what I want. He hooks his arm under my left knee, then the right, and braces himself against the wall as he fucks me hard.

"Shh," he whispers, but I have no control over my mouth. I risk taking one hand away from his back and shove a handful of silk shirt into my mouth as a gag. The Amsterdam police would not take kindly to our little display. Then I grab hold of Andreas again as I feel myself slip. He grunts as he heaves me higher and I give a muffled scream as he hits my cervix.

I glance across at the men. I feel sure one of them grunted when I screamed—*has he come already?* I notice they all have their dicks out now, but I no longer care. All I care about is Andreas and what he's doing to me.

He shifts his position slightly and I hit my head again as he finds that special spot—*G spot, A spot or is it the S spot?* I don't care what it's called; for me it's my Andreas spot. I didn't know it existed until I fucked him that first night.

Jolts of searing hot pleasure flood every inch of my body and I'm lost. Andreas' pounding grows stronger and harder and my back rasps against the brickwork—but I still don't care.

"Yes, yes, oh God, Andreas, yes!" My voice is so high-pitched it's almost a squeal as I come closer to ignition. I can hardly bear it. The sensation is too much; I need to come, I need to come now!

Andreas cries out as he plunges harder still and explodes inside me. I match him; my muscles spasming around him, drawing more orgasms from us both. Again and again we come, my own juices squirting with his, my shuddering in time with his.

Finally, we calm and look into each other's eyes, then kiss. I jerk as another spasm rips through my body and he throws his head back and cries out as my orgasm triggers another, just as powerful, in him.

My head falls forward onto his shoulder and he gently lowers my legs to the ground. They're trembling so much, I can hardly stand.

Applause breaks through our stupor and we both look toward the group of men that seems to have doubled in number. Andreas takes a bow, pants around his ankles, and I blow them a kiss; my shirt hanging open, my bra pushed up above my tits, and my skirt bunched around my waist. I have never looked more of a sight—and I bet not one of them will ever forget that image.

3

"Show's over," Andreas calls and tugs my skirt down. I smirk at him; it's a bit late for modesty now. However, I pull my bra back down over my breasts, taking my time over adjusting it until I'm comfortable, then hold both sides of my shirt open and laugh. "I've no buttons left."

Andreas looks so guilty I want to fuck him again, right away. "How are we going to get home? You can't walk the streets of Amsterdam like that at this time of night." He looks nervously at the men at the mouth of the alley. "I'd never get you past them for a start."

I grasp his face and kiss him, then take my shirttails and knot them just below my breasts.

"Gorgeous," he says, trailing a finger down my deep cleavage. "Now let's get you home."

Walking toward over a dozen men, all with their pants open, some with dicks still hard enough to point at me, should have been terrifying. But I've never felt scared with Andreas at my side. Over six feet tall, black, bald and with muscles honed in the gym as well as our bed, he looks as if he could take them all on if need be and barely raise a sweat.

I can't take my eyes off all the cocks as we approach. In a way, I've just fucked every one of them, too.

They part to let us through as we reach them and I

stifle a giggle. I'm reminded of an old film we watched at the weekend—a bride and groom passing through a tunnel of raised swords as they exited the church. I prefer this display.

Once through, I can't resist. I bend, lift the back of my skirt and wriggle my naked ass at them.

"Enough!" Andreas says, laughing. "I really don't want to have to fight them all off you!"

I laugh and smooth my skirt back down. "I feel like another drink and a joint—I think the last one's worn off."

"Bloody hell, Liesel, what's got into you tonight?"

I glance behind me and shrug. "Things have been tough lately. This is the first night out we've had for ages, and it's been amazing—I don't want it to end. Not yet."

"We can't afford it."

"I don't care. I want one night without worrying. Without scrimping. I want to be us again."

Andreas stops and pulls me into his arms. "I'm sorry, Liesel. You deserve better than this. I'll find work again soon."

"I know you will. It's not your fault, it's just life. It's hard for everyone at the moment. But let's just let go tonight, eh? Forget it all and enjoy."

"Are you sure?"

"Yes." I wrap my arms around his neck and kiss my husband. "I love you. Whatever's to come, we'll get through it. We'll be okay as long as we make some playtime." I giggle and bat my eyelashes.

"You know your eye makeup's all over your face, don't you?"

I laugh loudly and wipe my eyes. "Better?"

"Much, but you've missed a bit." He rubs the top of my cheek and kisses the tip of my nose, then leads me into a coffee shop. "Which flavor joint will it be this time, Liesel?"

I giggle and point at one of the glass jars behind the bar. "Let's try that one."

4

"It's weird, I should be exhausted, but I'm not tired," I say as we walk in through our front door.

"I know, me too."

"At least neither of us has to be up in the morning." I giggle, trying to make light of the stark truth that neither of us can find work.

"Just as well, considering it's past dawn!"

I lead the way into the kitchen and shake a bottle of vodka. "Another?"

"Yes please, just a small one though. Do you have a lighter?" Andreas asks, taking a joint from his pocket.

"When did you get that?" I almost squeal. In this fucked-up city you can smoke cannabis in the coffee shops, but nowhere else.

In answer, he just smiles and makes a flicking motion with his thumb. "After the earlier 'effects', I wanted some takeout."

I throw him a lighter and prepare the drinks, then follow him through to the sitting room.

Sitting close on the sofa, we clink glasses and both say, "Drink!" at the same time, laughing again. Neither of us is superstitious, but we're not prepared to risk seven years of bad sex.

Andreas lights the joint and breathes deeply before passing it to me.

"Tonight's been wonderful," I say, resting my head on his broad shoulder and passing the joint back.

"It's certainly been interesting," he counters. "What was that in the alley?"

"Wonderful," I repeat and giggle. "It's been far too long, I guess we overcompensated."

He laughs. "That's one way of putting it! But you're right, it's been too long. We've let our problems overcome . . . everything."

I say nothing. Andreas has been beyond sensitive ever since he was laid off from Schiphol. He's been blaming himself for our current financial situation—and taking it out on me. I hold my hand out for the joint.

"It was like when we first met again—only better."

He puts his arm around my shoulder, pulls me closer, and bends his head, but not for a kiss. Instead, he sucks in the fragrant smoke I exhale. *Then* he kisses me. "I love you, Liesel."

"I love you, too. And whatever happens, we'll be okay."

"I hope so."

I can think of no more to say so reach for my glass and take a drink. Andreas plucks the joint from between my fingers and I smile, but feel a little deflated. I really don't want the night to end on a bad note.

"I'm sorry," he says, and I hold my fingers to his mouth to shush him.

"It's not your fault," I assure him—although in a way it is. "As long as we're together, we'll be fine." I repeat the mantra.

He doesn't answer, but takes a long drag on the joint

before handing it to me and yawning.

I puff, then stub it out. "Come on, time for bed." I stand up and hold out my hand. Thankfully, he grins, takes it, stands and hugs me tight.

"Come on then."

I follow him to the bedroom and click on the light.

"Another bloody party," he says, indicating the window that looks onto the building behind ours. Even at 6 a.m. the apartment is full, the music blaring.

"Don't," I say, catching hold of his hand and stopping him from crossing to the window to shut the drapes.

He turns back to me. "This is new," he says, a smile tweaking the corners of his mouth.

"I know," I say, embarrassed. "That—in the alley— was amazing. I didn't realize I'm such an exhibitionist." I laugh, unsure how to go on.

"I like it," he says, kissing me and untying the knot of my shirt.

"Are you sure? I don't want . . ." I lose the rest of the sentence in his kiss and my shirt falls to the carpet.

"I like it," he repeats.

I kiss him again and relax. I pull his t-shirt out of his jeans and lift it. He raises his arms and breaks the kiss so I can pull it over his head. Then he turns us around so we're side-on to the window. Both of us are in full view.

I reach behind me and unclasp my bra, slowly drop the straps down my arms, then shrug it off. I hold it in my right outstretched hand—toward the window—and drop it.

Andreas smiles and leans in for another kiss, his hands on my breasts. I put my own hands on my lower back to brace myself before throwing my head back—heaven, no brick wall!—and push my chest up and into his hands. I almost go too far and grab his biceps to stop myself falling.

He laughs. "Relax, forget about the window and enjoy," he whispers, then bends his head to my breasts.

I move my hands to the back of his neck and head, and do as he instructs. I lose myself in the sensations of his tongue on one nipple, then the other. I reach behind me and undo the zipper of my skirt and let Andreas tug it down. It falls to the floor, leaving me clad only in stockings.

I step back. I need to stop this so I can undress him too. His body is far too sculpted to be hidden by cotton.

I pull his belt open again, unfasten his jeans, and push them down with his boxers. While he bends to pull them and his socks off, I glance toward the window. We've been noticed.

"Alright?" He's upright again and has spotted my interest.

"Oh yes," I say and kneel in front of him. I lick at the milky liquid already on the tip of his cock, taking him into my mouth. He's too big for me to take his full length, so I close my fist around him too and start to pump—hand and mouth working perfectly together.

"Oh God, Liesel," he hisses, thrusting his hips into my face. I lick and suck as I withdraw, knowing from experience he can't take much more of this. I want more. And more. *And more*.

I stand, my hand still stroking his cock and walk backwards, pulling him to the bed. I lift one leg up, then the other until I'm kneeling in front of him, and release his cock as I shuffle backwards. He crawls onto the bed after me and I push him sideways so that he rolls onto his back.

I straddle him, lean down to kiss him and tease the tip of his cock with my clitoris, circling it, then move until he's pressing against the entrance to my vagina.

I straighten, rest my hands against his belly, then slowly lower my body, skewering myself onto him. I push down as far as I can, then rotate my hips with him deep, deep inside me. I gasp in pleasure and he grasps my hips, lifting me. I rise, then plummet down on him, both of us crying out, then again, and again, and again . . .

5

My legs are shaking and I grab his right hand from my hip with my left. Then his left with my right. Fingers interlocked together, I push off him to keep going, to keep pumping, to keep the piston inside me firing.

But my legs can't do it; I have no strength left, I've used it all. With a powerful thrust, Andreas lifts me and pushes me to the side, rolling with me, staying inside me, and takes over.

I lift my shaking legs with my hands, pulling them up so my knees are by my ears, my ankles under his armpits, and scream with the intensity of the sensation of his thrusts.

I lose all sense of time, all sense of the world, even all sense of the people watching. All that exists is his cock, my vagina, his groans, my moans. I scream as I orgasm, then over and over again. I have ejaculated before, but never like this, never as much as this, never as often as this. I must be squirting pints of juice onto our bed, and can't stop. My body is no longer flesh and bone but pure energy, pure sensation: heat, searing flame, electric shocks, every nerve ending alive and screaming in joy. My nerve endings, and his too; my voice, his too.

Finally he collapses, exhausted, next to me, and I can't imagine moving, even though the bed sheets are soaked. I turn to the window; it's a sea of faces, most cheering, although some look uncomfortable.

I roll onto my side and get up from the bed, then stroll towards the glass. I reach out to grasp the drapes and hold the pose a moment before pulling them closed and turning back to Andreas. He's on his side on the bed, propping himself up on one elbow.

He raises an eyebrow and says, "I have an idea. I think I know how we can solve all our problems and keep the apartment."

"How?" I ask.

"Not now," he says. "We'll talk later when you're sober. Now come back to bed."

He lifts the blanket and wriggles underneath, holding it up for me. I climb in and snuggle up to him. The past few months have been hell, but the future is definitely looking up.

6

"Morning."

I open my eyes then immediately squeeze them shut—to Andreas' laughter. The enticing smell of fresh coffee makes me squint them open again, and I prop myself up on one elbow.

"What time is it?"

"About half two."

"What?" I open my eyes fully again. A mistake. I reach for the coffee and sip. It burns my mouth and I put it down, lie back and pull the covers over my head.

After a moment, light strikes my eyelids as Andreas lifts the covers to climb in next to me. I roll over to him as he holds my waist and pulls me close.

"Last night was amazing."

"Yes." I smile into his chest. "Crazy!"

He kisses the top of my head and I bend my neck back so I can kiss him properly. The drapes are still closed.

"Do you want me to open them?" he asks, teasing me.

"No. Don't think I can put on much of a show today." I feel my face burn with the ferocity of my blush. I can't believe we fucked in full view of the neighbors.

"They won't be neighbors long," Andreas said. "We haven't paid the rent in two months, we'll be evicted soon."

I don't know whether to smile at him for knowing

what I was thinking, or cry for the situation we're in.

"I love you," he says and kisses me. Grateful for the respite from my embarrassment, I kiss him back, despite my no doubt horrendous morning mouth.

"Are you okay?"

"Yes," I reply. "Embarrassed, but to be honest, it was so hot!"

He laughs. "I thought I knew everything there was to know about you, but you certainly surprised me."

"I surprised myself," I mumble, my face in his chest again. I remember the men watching us in the alley and squeeze my legs together, unsure what to think about the flood of feeling and moisture that has just overtaken me. Then I remember the neighbors at the window—*how can I ever face them again?*

"You said last night you have an idea."

"Umm, forget it. It seemed a good one last night—this morning," he corrects himself. "Not so much now."

"No, tell me."

"Er, okay, well . . ." He breaks off. Now I really want to know what it is.

"Um. Well, you know how you liked people watching?"

I giggle, nervously. "Yeah. Oh my God, didn't you like it? I'm so sorry—I just got carried away."

"No, no, I liked it—I loved having people watch me make love to you. I felt so special—you could have had any one of them, but you wanted me."

"Absofuckinglutely," I say and kiss him. "You're the love of my life, the only man I'll ever want—"

"Yeah, yeah," he says, embarrassed, and I grit my teeth. I hate that he can't accept how much I love him, and worry a little that he never says I'm the only woman he'll ever want.

"Anyway," he continues, "The Theater Voyeur is looking for a new act—"

"How do you know that?" Now I'm more angry than worried.

"Wulf told me. He's a stagehand there."

"Oh." Of course. They'd been at school together; he was a bit creepy but harmless enough.

"What do you think about doing a show?"

"What? Us? Having sex on stage?"

"Well, yes. It wouldn't be much different from what we did last night, and the money's fantastic"

"But . . . wouldn't that be prostitution?"

"No! Of course not—we'd only be fucking each other, no one else, but people would be paying to watch, that's all. Remember that alley? And the neighbors' party?" He glances toward the window.

I stay silent. My head's screaming "No", but I'm as wet as fuck.

"Could we do it, though, on demand like that? What if we get stage fright?"

"At the end of the day—night—it would just be us, loving each other. We can try it, and if it doesn't work, well, no harm done."

I turn, pick up my coffee and drink. We're out of options. Neither of us has been able to find a job, we're about to lose the apartment; if we don't do something drastic we'll end up on the street. I shudder at the thought of what that might entail. But a sex show?

"Liesel?"

I put the mug down and turn back to him. "Okay."

1

"Are you sure you want to do this?" Andreas asks.

I look into the dressing-room mirror surrounded by light bulbs—some working, most not—and wonder why it's called a dressing room when most of our clothes have come off. My face is so made-up I'm a caricature of a woman, barely recognizable. Lola. That's my stage name. That's the woman who looks out at me, the woman preparing to fuck "Darcy" in public.

I wear a red silk robe and have on only a skimpy, barely-there black lace negligee underneath. I take another deep drag of my joint, meet Andreas' eyes in the mirror and nod. I don't trust my voice—I'm terrified.

He steps closer, wraps his arms around me and nuzzles my neck. "We don't have to, you know."

I think of the auditorium. Is it full or are there only a handful of dirty old men out there? Will there be any women? "Yes, we do. They're paying us €500, we need that money. It'll keep the landlord quiet for a month at least.

Andreas' hand moves down from my waist, slips between the folds of my robe, and cups my pubis. "I love you bare." I've had a full body wax; the only hair I still sport is on my head.

He parts the folds of my cleft and pushes his finger

further down. "Oh my God, you're so wet!"

I grind my buttocks into his groin—his cock is like a wooden club against my asshole. He circles my clit with his fingertip and I groan, tilting my pelvis to give him better access.

He bends me forward so he can reach further and pushes his finger into me. I widen my legs and he pushes a second finger in, then a third. I lift a knee onto the counter, displaying myself in the mirror for us both to watch. The pink skin glistens and I'm transfixed by the sight of his hand working.

"No need to ask if you two are ready."

Andreas and I gasp and my eyes meet Wulf's in the mirror. I didn't hear the door open.

Andreas' fingers—stilled at the interruption—start working again. I don't take my eyes off Wulf—whose attention is focused on my vagina.

Andreas resumes his finger movements and my eyes flick up to his reflected face—he's watching Wulf, and I turn my own gaze back. His pants bulge gratifyingly and I push my knees further apart, forcing myself further onto Andreas' fingers.

Wulf licks his lips and stares.

Then Andreas focuses his actions on my G-spot and I explode.

"You might want to save that for the show, you're on in five," Wulf says, then leaves. The door is slow to close and we hear clearly his "Fucking amateurs" before it shuts.

I look at Andreas and we laugh before he helps me get my foot back down to the floor.

"Ready?"

"Ready." I grin. I am. No matter who's watching, I just want Andreas inside me.

8

My nerves are back. Standing in the wings, behind the still-closed curtain, looking at the large circular bed swathed in red satin to match our robes, I realize this is it. The moment of no return is fast approaching.

Music, interspersed with women's groans, reverberates around the Theater Voyeur. It's full; apparently fresh blood is hotly anticipated here. Two hundred people—at least 90 percent men, though probably more—are gathered to watch us have sex.

A gesture from the stage manager, Detlef, is accompanied by a push from behind. Time to take our places.

Andreas takes my hand and leads me to the bed. He kisses me. "If it's too much and you want to stop, it's no problem," he tells me. And I know he means it. My vagina waters.

I clamber onto the bed—my back to the curtain—and position myself upright on my knees. Wulf arranges my robe around me. My chest is covered, but there's a glimpse of my negligee just skirting my groin before the robe flares around my legs and circles around me on the bed.

Andreas kisses his fingers then presses them against my lips. "You look beautiful, Liesel," he whispers.

"Enjoy this."

He walks offstage with Wulf and I'm alone with the curtain about to open at any moment.

♥

The music fades and a new beat resounds. Primal, urgent and sexy as hell. Rihanna's *S&M*. My heart hammers in fear and anticipation.

I throw my head back to let my hair cascade down my back and take a deep breath.

The curtains open.

Silence.

The spotlight flares and a roar of approval hits my ears. My eyes slide sideways to see Andreas blow me a kiss, and the bed starts to revolve.

As it moves, I undo the belt of my robe with shaking fingers, shrug it free from my shoulders, hold it to my breast and freeze as I move side-on to the audience.

Then I'm turned to face them and think, *What the hell.* I drop my robe and my hands move of their own accord to cover my groin.

I can see no one, but know they're there. For a moment I panic. Two hundred people! But a tingling between my legs helps, and then Andreas, in his matching robe, strides onto the stage and I smile. I *will* enjoy this. But I can't move my hands away.

Anticipation turns the tingle to raw heat, and for a moment I forget I'm on a stage, forget about the people watching me—no doubt with bated breath waiting for me to move my hands and their cocks freed from pants. My whole being is focused on the expectation of Andreas reaching me, touching me, fucking me.

The bed stops moving.

I'm kneeling, pelvis thrust forward wearing the thin negligee, spotlight focused on my body—four hundred *eyes* focused on my body—and all I'm aware of is Andreas behind me.

The audience calls for me to move my hands, but I'm not ready yet, then they cheer and I know Andreas has shed his robe, leaving his magnificent brown, oiled body completely nude, although hidden behind me—for the moment.

He places his hands either side of my face and I arch back to him. His fingers slide down my neck, across my shoulders, and push the straps of my negligee down my arms. I groan.

His hands move across my body to my breasts, stroking and kneading them, teasing my nipples through the negligee. Then he grabs the lace in two fists and rips.

9

Andreas' hands return to my breasts and take up their familiar rhythm, and I thrust my chest out, surrendering to him, leaning my head back to rest on his shoulder.

His fingers move lower—slowly, ever so slowly—stroking my belly, then my hips. He strokes his hands over mine and gently moves them away. The audience gasps with me.

His right hand moves inward and I push my hips out to meet it. I know I'm displaying myself to hundreds of strangers' eyes, but I can't help myself. They only make my need more urgent and I moan as his fingers find my clit.

My hips buck once, twice, again and again as he brings me to my first orgasm—well, apart from the one in the dressing room. For a brief moment I wonder if anyone in the audience comes too.

The bed turns again and Andreas pushes me between the shoulder blades. I catch myself on my hands and kneel, doggy-style, before him. The crowd cheers and I smile. I'm enjoying this now. Who has so many men desiring them at once? And I'm only making love to the man I love.

The bed stops moving and I feel Andreas' cock nudge my cleft. I spread my legs and have to look away from the bright lights at the foot of the stage. I close my eyes; at this point, the only man I want to be aware of is Andreas.

He pushes into me, but only a fraction before pulling out again, and I open my eyes in surprise to see the entire back wall of the stage is now a gigantic LED screen—filled with Andreas' magnificent, huge black cock, and my wet pink, eager vagina.

I twitch my hips and watch his cock plunge into me. I cry out—a cry echoed throughout the auditorium—and press my hips to his, then grind against him. He pulls out and I'm captivated by the sight of his glistening silky penis emerging from my depths.

I scream as he skewers me again, losing all awareness other than the sensations in my vagina, spreading heat throughout my body.

On and on the pounding goes, and I start to worry. I've already come more times than I can count, and there is no let up. I grow more aware of the audience and try to brace my body into a semblance of sexiness, but I'm a quivering wreck. And Andreas is showing no traces of tiring—or coming. The voyeurs that so excite me seem to inspire some kind of pride in him: he has to keep going, longer than any of them can.

I start to pray as I launch into yet another multiple orgasm, darkening the satin sheets with my juices. *They'll have to be thrown away,* I think, yelping as another orgasm even bigger than before rips through me.

I collapse, my knees and elbows like jelly, and no longer able to hold me up.

Andreas doesn't falter and continues to plunge into me

as I lie face down on the soaking sheets.

I turn my face away from the screen and look out into the lights. A very male, and collective, cry tells me they like seeing me, and I build to yet another climax.

The music swells and crescendos and I realize Andreas is ready to do the same. I push my hips up, desperate for him to come. Desperate to come with him.

His thrusts become more urgent and less measured, and I realize he's close.

"Yes, Andreas, yes, come on, fuck me, I want you to come so badly, come on, fill me . . ."

My words tail off as he explodes—I can physically feel his cock pulse inside me as he comes—and the ferocity of my accompanying orgasm—and scream—winds me.

We collapse in a heap as the lights go dark and the curtains close.

Another Rihanna song, *What's My Name?* reverberates around the theater then it fades and Detlef's voice is magnified over it. "Her name's Lola, gentlemen. Show your appreciation for Lola and Darcy!"

Silence, and for a moment I'm worried—but then, what do I expect? Applause? It isn't that kind of show.

Then I hear grunts and cries and embarrassed laughter, and Andreas chuckles in my ear. We're both beyond words.

"Oh my God, you guys were fantastic!" Wulf has rushed onto the stage and doesn't seem at all fazed by the fact we're both naked and Andreas is still inside me.

Andreas grunts. I don't react, I'm not capable.

"Detlef wants to give you a permanent contract—four

times a week: Monday, Wednesday, Friday and Saturday—€1000 a show. He wants DVDs, a TV show, the works! This is fantastic!"

"Fifty percent of all sales," Andreas says, and I laugh, but not in humor. *Can I do this four times a week?*

10

Andreas opens the stage door for me and I step out into the chill night air, then take a quick pace backwards as a camera flash blinds me.

"Liesel? Are you okay?"

"Yes, yes, just caught by surprise, that's all."

Andreas steps around me to berate the photographer, but a show flyer is thrust into his face, along with a pen.

"That was fantastic—can I have your autographs?"

"Oh, er, right, yes of course." He scrawls the name Darcy, then passes the flyer to me.

My eyes have recovered from the flash and I realize half a dozen men—no, more—are gathered around the stage door. I pause after the *L* and remember to write Lola then hand the flyer back and another is thrust at me. I wince as someone else takes a picture and feel very uncomfortable. These men have seen every part of me, have watched me come. I enjoyed it on the stage, when they were eyes in the gloom, the other side of the stage lights and at a distance. Here they're too close; touching me, calling my name and taking my picture.

Once we've signed half a dozen flyers, the men melt away—apart from one who passes his cellphone to Andreas.

"Can you take a picture of me with her, mate? It would mean so much."

I squint at him; he looks to be in his forties, quite respectable-looking, and at least clean. White, with a strong jaw, dark hair and a bit of stubble.

"Lola?" Andreas asks.

I shake my head and step closer to him. I don't like this at all.

"Sorry, man, not tonight, this is all a bit much."

"Oh, right, I get it. I'm good enough for you to take my money and flash your cunt, but no touching, eh?"

"You little shit!" Andreas lunges at him, but the man is too quick and runs.

Andreas moves to go after him, but I grab his arm. "Don't leave me!"

He hesitates, then hugs me. "Sorry, Liesel, I didn't think . . . I didn't expect . . ."

"I know. Me neither. I just feel a bit . . . vulnerable."

"I know, I know, sorry. We'll make sure it doesn't happen again, I'll have a word with Wulf, get some security on the door."

I nod and sniff.

"Hey, there's no need to cry, no one will hurt you. They'd have to get through me first!"

"Yeah, I know. It's just all a bit overwhelming. Can we go home?"

"Of course, come on, the car's just round the corner."

♥

"Do you want a drink?"

"No." I shake my head. "I just want to go to bed—I'm exhausted."

"Yeah, me too. It was quite a night wasn't it?"

I laugh. "You can say that again."

"I don't think I've ever seen you looking sexier, kneeling on that bed, waiting for the curtain to open."

I smile, thinking back to that moment. I'd been petrified, yet had never felt so alive—or wet. Every nerve in my body had been on fire thinking about what we were about to do.

Andreas bends his head and kisses me, slowly and tenderly. The urgency of the rest of the evening dissipates.

I wrap my arms around his neck and stand on tiptoe to return his kiss, squealing when he bends, hooks one arm under my knees, the other under my shoulders, picks me up and carries me to the bedroom.

He lays me gently on the bed, then glances at the window. "Open or closed?" He smirks.

"Closed." I smile up at him. "Just you and me."

He crosses to the window and draws the drapes, then turns back to me, pulling his t-shirt over his head. I prop myself up on my elbows to watch him strip, subconsciously licking my lips as his gorgeous body is slowly revealed. Well-developed shoulders and chest, now hairless—he'd also subjected himself to a waxing. Taut, muscled belly. His hands pause at his belt, teasing me. I lift my eyes to his and he grins, reading my desire.

My eyes flick back down as he undoes his belt and button, then slowly draws the zipper down. He's not wearing boxers and his cock springs forward as soon as he pushes his jeans down. The thickness of my wrist and length near enough that of my forearm, I nearly come just at the sight of him and I clutch the hem of my dress.

He walks quickly to the bed and grabs my hands. "Let me."

I defer to him and lie back. He pushes the skirt up and I lift my hips so he can slide the thin material past my ass, then sit up and lift my arms so he can pull it clear of my body.

He reaches behind me and unclasps my bra, then grabs the front with his teeth. I fall back to the bed, leaving the lace behind. He drops it to the side, then bends and nuzzles my breasts—licking and nipping my nipples, knowing just how hard to bite. Jolts of fire flow to my groin and I moan.

He moves lower and hooks his thumbs into the flimsy sides of my thong. I lift my hips again, but he grins, pulling the lace apart. I gasp in pleasant surprise.

He spreads my legs and runs a finger down my cleft, then uses his thumbs to spread my lips apart. He pauses, stares at me and I squirm—I love him looking at me so intimately, but want more.

Bending his head, his tongue flicks my clit and I jerk, already so close to coming. He swirls his tongue around my tiny organ, which is already so sensitive I don't think I can stand it. But I want more and thrust against his mouth. His tongue moves lower, teasing the entrance to my vagina, and I use my hands to pull my aching legs further apart.

He moves his hands to my buttocks and lifts me as his tongue swirls and probes and licks.

I squeal as my juices squirt into his mouth and he drinks. He moves up the bed to kiss me. "I love it when you do that—you taste gorgeous!" I lap at his mouth, sharing the taste of my most intimate place.

I lift my knees and tilt my hips. His cock pushes against my vagina and I moan, wanting him inside me—now! But he still wants to tease and circles his hips; playing with me, toying with my need.

"Andreas, please . . ." I gasp.

He giggles and kisses me. "I love it when you beg."

"Please, Andreas, I want you so badly." I don't care that I'm begging. If he doesn't fuck me soon, I won't be accountable for my actions.

Recognizing I'm sore, he pushes in gently, filling me completely and finding "his spot" first time and I whimper as another orgasm rips through me.

I pull my knees up, bracing them between his shoulders and mine, grab his ass, and he rocks, knowing well the rhythm that suits us both so well.

I'm completely lost in him, in the sensation of his cock stroking the walls of my vagina, hitting that sweet spot over and over again.

My screams become uncontrollable as I orgasm again and again, squirting my juice over his cock, his balls, and God knows where else.

"Oh my God, Liesel!" he shouts, pushing in hard and holding himself there as he comes, our spasms wringing even more orgasms from each other.

Eventually we calm, and he kisses me then starts to withdraw. "Oh!" I squeal as another burst of heat explodes through me.

"Christ!" Andreas cries, shuddering. "I can't fucking stop coming!"

I'm incapable of words and make only unintelligible cries as we stay locked together, our bodies out of control: bucking, jerking, coming.

Eventually he collapses on top of me and rolls over. We look at each other, panting hard, words still beyond us. He strokes my cheek tenderly, and smiles. I nod. Yes, I love him too

.

11

"Goede morgen, lieveling."

"Morgen, Andreas."

I put the bags on the kitchen counter and pull out fresh rolls, still warm, then orange juice and Pflaumenmus—the damson jam Andreas loves so much.

He moves behind me, embraces me and nuzzles my neck. I stiffen.

"What's wrong?" He puts pressure on my shoulder, encouraging me to turn. But I resist. "Liesel?"

"That man—the creepy one from the theater—he was there, outside the baker's."

"What? Are you sure?"

"Yes, of course I'm fucking sure!" I turn around to face him. "He was there, watching me, waiting for me to come back out. He took a fucking photo on his damn phone!"

"Liesel . . ." He tries to hug me, but I push him away.

"I don't like it, Andreas. It's one thing on the stage or in that alley, when they're anonymous, but this guy isn't anonymous anymore."

"Did he follow you?"

"What? Oh my God, I don't know. What if he knows where we live?" Now I did let him hold me.

"It'll be okay, we're celebrities now. You have a fan." He laughs.

"It's not fucking funny. This guy watched us have sex. Now he's watching me, following me!"

"Mm. It's not good, but I'm sure he's harmless—he just likes to look, that's all. He's not going to hurt you."

I push him away. "How the fuck do you know? We've no idea who he is or what he's capable of."

He stays quiet a moment, then his shoulders sag. "You're right, we can't take any chances. We're about to be evicted anyway—the money we got last night isn't enough for a deposit for a new place, but by next week we'll have enough for both deposit and rent, we'll find somewhere else in a different area. We'll start looking today. Somewhere with security. We'll be fine, but you're right, we need to be careful now."

I move into his arms again. "Thank you," I mumble into his chest.

"We'll start apartment hunting straight after breakfast."

I nod, hold him a moment, then move to prepare the meal.

♥

"Look! There he is—he *did* follow me!"

We're just about to get in the car—a battered Mini, barely legal—and I spot the creep across the street. He waves.

"Andreas!"

Andreas bolts straight across the road, knocking some guy off his bike. They collapse in a heap and narrowly miss being hit by another half-dozen bicycles. By the time they pick themselves up, the man's gone.

"Come on, Liesel." Andreas re-joins me. "He's gone, it's safe."

I nod and get into the car.

♥

"Andreas, it's gorgeous," I breathe. Overlooking the Keizersgracht Canal, with high ceilings and big rooms—*three* bedrooms—it also boasts security at the gate to the compound. "But can we afford it?"

"We will be able to next week, lieveling. Four shows a week at €1000 a show, not to mention the other stuff. Get used to this, Liesel. You deserve the best, and now it's finally come. We'll take it," he adds to the realtor.

"Wonderful. If you'd like to keep looking around, I'll fetch the paperwork from the office, I'll be ten minutes."

Andreas waves at the man, then grins at me. "He thought we were time-wasters; he didn't even bring the contract!"

"Well, look at us!" We're both wearing worn jeans; Andreas with another t-shirt, me in a faded cotton shirt. "We hardly fit the usual picture of his clientele."

"Hmm, well, you do make quite a picture though." He makes a show of licking his lips, reaches out and slowly pops my top button.

"Andreas, we can't. He'll be back soon!"

"So?" He arches an eyebrow and my mouth twitches. He has a point.

My next button parts from its buttonhole, then the next and the next until my shirt is hanging open.

I stand there, passive, letting Andreas do whatever he wants to me. It's agony to keep my arms at my sides—I want to rip his clothes away from his body—but I know my self-discipline will be well rewarded.

He eases my shirt from my shoulders and steps back to look me up and down.

"Um hmm, nice. But could be better."

He steps forward again, unsnaps my jeans and pushes them from my hips, then all the way down. He kneels, lifts my right leg to ease off my sneaker, sock and pants leg, then the same for my left.

Standing, he takes a pace back and admires the view. A matching pale-pink bra and string set—all lace. I know what Andreas likes.

He quickly rids himself of his own clothes then reaches for me, stroking my arms, waist and back, until he finds the clasp of my bra. It joins the rest of my clothes on the floor, and is quickly followed by my panties. He licks his lips and stares.

I'm trembling with the effort of not reacting to him, but I love him looking at me like this. Eyes black, muscles taut, cock reaching for me.

My hands, which are resting on my hips, elbows cocked, move inwards. I spread my legs and slowly stroke myself. Softly at first, then harder.

I let my right hand continue and move my left to my breasts. I throw my head back and moan.

"Oh God, Liesel." He moves to me quickly, pushes me backwards until I'm resting against the wall, and spins me around.

I support myself with my hands, move my feet back and brace, pushing my ass out in invitation. He grabs my hips, takes a moment to position himself, then stabs into me. I scream.

There's no more build up—we don't have long after all—and he thrusts hard and fast. I love it.

I push against him harder, bending lower and screaming again as the full power of him brutalizes my sensitive flesh. "Oh God, Andreas, yes!"

He's taken me from naught to sixty in seconds and I'm incapable of doing anything to help. Every stab wrings sensations from me so exquisite it's almost painful; almost.

"Ahem."

Fuck, the realtor's back!

"Just a minute, man," Andreas says.

I think about the picture we must present: both naked, Andreas' every muscle working hard and well-defined, me bent almost double, my tits swinging, covered in sweat, groaning without filter.

Andreas thrusts harder, and I cry out—he's never fucked me this hard from behind before. I don't know how much I can take. Then, with a final sustained thrust, his full length pushing into every crevice of my vagina, I feel his spasms push me over the edge of the cliff I'm teetering on. I shriek, now completely unaware of the man watching. *How has this become normal so quickly?*

We stay there a few more moments as further, gentler, spasms wrack our bodies, then Andreas slowly pulls out.

His arm around my waist pulls me upright and I turn to the doorway. "Where do we sign?" I ask.

12

I pour oil into my palm and rub it into Andreas' back, gently stroking every inch of his skin, then move around him to give his arms, chest and belly the same treatment. I know he's watching me but I can't meet his eyes—I can't take my gaze away from his body, from watching my hands spread the glistening emollient over his beautiful skin.

I turn to get more oil, kneel to rub it into his feet and legs, then I move upwards, circling his thighs, kneading his ass.

His cock bumps my face. I have deliberately left this part of him till last. I notice a drop of milky liquid on the tip, and lick it off with a moan, massaging his balls with my slick hands as I take him into my mouth.

"Liesel, oh God. No, stop, wait. I need to last out there—I can't if you do this to me now."

I smile and withdraw, using my hands to lubricate him instead. He grabs my upper arms and pulls me back up to stand in front of him. "Stop teasing," he says. "Save it for the stage."

"My turn," I answer. He grins and fills his hands with oil, then turns me to anoint my back, buttocks and the backs of my legs. He turns me back around and pushes me against the counter.

His hands stroke my shoulders and arms, then my

chest. He spends some time making sure every pore of my breasts is properly oiled, then moves down to my belly. He skirts my groin and attends to the fronts of my legs—even my feet—then nudges them apart and looks up at me. Not at my face, but at my groin.

I tilt my pelvis, teasing his eyes, and say, "What happened to saving it for the show?"

"*I* need to save it for the show or I won't be able to perform. *You,* on the other hand, need to be *prepared* for the show. I want you wet and desperate from the moment the curtain rises."

I throw my head back and laugh, pushing my pelvis further towards him and his mouth immediately smothers me.

His tongue licks as far back as he can reach, moving forward until he finds my clit, which he circles, licks, sucks and gently nips.

I gasp and groan, pushing harder against him and his tongue pushes into my vagina. "Oh God, Andreas, that's so good!"

He pulls out and stands up, and I protest. *Don't stop now!*

He takes a little more oil, moves his hand between my legs and strokes, covering my clitoris with oil, then moves lower until his fingers, still slippery, find the opening to my vagina. He slips one finger in, cocking it to tickle the sensitive spot just inside.

My body jerks once, twice, three times, building to a crescendo.

He grins and kisses me, his other hand grasping my breast, as he slips a second finger in and twists.

I break the kiss to breathe, throw my head back again, and spread my legs further.

A third finger enters and I moan. He pulls out, pushes in, back and forth, twisting his hand one way then the other.

Groaning, feeling the pressure build inside me, I want more.

I lift my right leg up and he grabs the back of it, just above the knee, pushing it up and out. His hand speeds up and I can barely brace myself against the countertop anymore. My hips buck, pushing his hand even deeper and he starts to move quickly: faster and faster until I explode with a ferocity that surprises us both.

He grins, removes his hand and licks his fingers. "Ready now?"

"Oh shit, Andreas, this is crazy."

"Yes, crazy wonderful."

I nod, and lean forward to rest against him.

13

Standing in the wings wearing my robe, I grab hold of Andreas' hand. I look up at him nervously, conflicting emotions coursing through me. Satisfaction, craving for more, anticipation, fear. I peek out at the audience. The theater is full. People—men—are even standing at the back. I shudder—*is the creep here tonight?*

"Don't worry, Liesel, you'll love it when we get out there, you know you will."

I look up at him and smile. He's right, I *will* love it. I think back to the last show and that night in the alley, and lick my lips. Then I remember the face of the realtor the other day; his expression shocked and embarrassed, yet unable to tear his eyes away. I remember how natural it felt, how much I liked him looking at us, desiring me, yet unable to touch me. I realize I don't care if that creep *is* in the audience—as long as he stays there.

"On you go," Wulf says. "Thirty seconds."

We walk onto the stage and toward the bed—this time dressed in white. We shrug off our robes, push them under the platform and get into position.

"Three, two, one," Wulf calls from the wings, barely audible over the music. The curtains swish open as a new track plays—Kings of Leon, *Sex on Fire*—and the spot lights us up.

We're in profile to the auditorium, the LED screen

playing brief spurts of footage from our previous show, interspersed with images of flames and flowers (orchids of course). A little clichéd, but very suitable.

Andreas lies on his back and I straddle him, my hands over my breasts, the tip of his cock just nudging my vagina, but from this position, only the men on the far left side of the room can see that.

I focus on Andreas' face as I hold the pose and smile down at him, my heart hammering once more. I am so excited I can barely wait for my music cue to plunge. *There it is.* I slowly sink onto him, my legs hurting from the effort. *I'm going to need to go to the gym and strengthen up.*

I grind against him, then lift myself up and down again, grind, up, down, grind.

My breathing comes faster and my legs start to shake.

Andreas grabs my ass and helps to lift me. I plummet down again—harder this time—then again, faster, *faster*.

"Yes, lieveling, yes, oh my God, that's good!' Andreas says, spurring me on.

I move my hands to his waist and arch my back. There's a smattering of applause as my breasts are revealed and the bed revolves until I'm facing my admirers. I stare out beyond the lights and let my eyes swing from left to right and back again. I can't see anyone for the glare, but I want every single one of those men to think I've looked at him while I fuck Andreas.

The bed moves again. I straighten and move my hands behind me, grabbing Andreas' thighs, and arch further. I glance at the back wall of the stage and the images being played on the enormous screen. A close-up of my face dominates it and I lick my lips, my eyes narrowed.

The camera moves down, focusing on my breasts bouncing up and down with the power of my thrusts. Then lower still, until my vagina and Andreas' cock are displayed twenty feet high.

I rise up, right to Andreas' tip and the camera zooms in, then I plunge on top of him, watching him be swallowed up inside me. I pull up again, and moan at the sight of his glistening black cock emerging from my depths.

Down again, and I cry out. *This is so incredibly hot!* I move faster and more urgently, and the bed revolves again. Now my back is to the audience. They can see for themselves Andreas' cock being submerged inside me— from both front and back. My eyes are transfixed on the screen as I fuck, screaming now every time I drop and Andreas reaches my special spot.

Faster and faster. I can see every vein in his cock. I can see the pink of my cleft, the darker red of my labia. I shriek my first orgasm, my hips bucking out of control, and barely hear the cheer in the crowd behind me. I'm engrossed in the sight of liquid spurting out of me, coating Andreas' cock and lower belly. *Oh my God, I want to do that again!* I don't stop my pounding, which becomes even fiercer.

Andreas cries out too and I've lost all control of my mouth: Harsh, primal screams are wrung out of me with every plummet, every jolt of fire bursting through me. I keep watching, and throw my head back with a howl when the hardest orgasm yet rips me apart.

I collapse on top of Andreas, only now realizing he came at the same moment. "Fucking hell, Liesel," he grunts.

The stage is plunged into darkness and the curtain closes. I notice there's no sound from the auditorium, not even the rustle of people leaving their seats. Then I understand: They're all busy.

14

"Fucking hell, guys, that was amazing!" Wulf rushes onto the stage, stopping sharply as noise bursts in on us from the theater.

"What the hell?"

A stamping; regular, loud and insistent, then cries of "More!"

Wulf looks at us in wonder for a moment, completely bewildered, then snaps into action. "Take a break. We'll do a double show tonight. Give me half an hour to collect another ticket price, then you're back on."

"What? Wulf, I can't! Bloody hell, what do you think I am? Did you not just see that?"

"Of course I fucking did, it was amazing. Liesel watching the screen like that—genius." He smacks my ass. I'm too exhausted to care.

"Here take one of these." He throws a small blue pill to Andreas. It'll get you back up and running in no time. And if it's not quick enough," he pauses and glances at me, "well, I'm sure you can think of something!"

"But half an hour, Wulf!"

"Ja. Half an hour, and another €1000. Get off the stage, clean yourselves up and have a nap if you need to. But make no mistake: this show is a hit; you're not walking away from it."

"No," I say, and Wulf turns white with panic.

"No, we won't walk away," I continue with a smile.

"Are you sure, Liesel?"

"Oh yes." I bend, kiss Andreas, then get off the bed and walk to the wings.

In the dressing room, I pour myself a vodka and tonic then light a joint. Only now do I realize I left my robe under the bed.

15

I'm alone on the stage when the curtain opens again an hour later. There are so many people who wanted to stay that their money couldn't be collected in only half an hour.

In a supine position on the round bed, my head rests on a pillow, my feet point to the audience. I'm wearing a strapless bra and string panties which Wulf had been sent out to procure.

Watching the camera above capture every bit of me, I'm very aware that the shot is being fed directly to the screen behind my head: my body—tits to groin—over my underwear, then back up to my tits. I toy with them, circle them, knead them, and caress my nipples through the lace.

I undo the front clasp of my bra and slowly, ever so slowly, pull the two halves apart. Catcalls and whistles shower approval on me and I smile, faltering when I think I hear my name being called. *No, it's my imagination—my nerves and senses are hyper-alert.*

I repeat my attentions to my now naked breasts, teasing my nipples with thumb and finger, and push and twist until they stand out like rocks—jewels—on my breasts.

Trailing my fingers slowly over my skin, I move lower

and slide them beneath the lace of my thong. I surprise myself at how wet I am. The camera whirs as it zooms in; I wish I could see the screen from here.

I hook a finger either side of my panties; the side straps have been weakened and one quick tug snaps them. I throw the scrap of lace toward the front of the stage.

A cheer and a rumbling chatter tell me I managed to get it past the lights and into the seats. When they settle, I slowly open my legs. More cheers. I gently rub my hands up and down my cleft, then play with my clit with one hand while I stroke my breasts with the other.

The camera moves forward and tilts to capture a better angle. That's my cue.

Moaning, I draw my knees up—still apart—until my feet are flat on the bed. I moan again and pull my lips apart, fully exposing my most intimate secrets to my audience, then slip a finger into myself; working it in and out quickly until my body spasms with an orgasm. Another cheer is accompanied by a revolution of the bed, and Andreas stands before me.

Smiling up at him as he crawls onto the bed, I remove my finger and slide a glance at the screen. He's licking my legs as he moves closer, then my clit. I whimper and buck, but I'm too far gone for this to work.

Groaning, I reach for him. He understands and moves further up the bed. My legs either side of him, he rears up and grinds his cock into my vagina.

I cry out and jerk my hips. With a nudge from Andreas, I remember to extend my legs, holding them up straight into the air, my toes pointed in their stilettos. *Yes, I definitely need a gym!*

Andreas pushes into me, gently now, and I moan and move with him, looking back at the screen, at his cock sliding out of me then pushing back in; a rhythm I know he can keep up longer than the length of a show—with or without a little blue pill.

I turn my head toward the audience and am rewarded with whistles. I smile and let my eyes wander before looking back up at Andreas.

His pounding becomes more urgent and his face is a grimace. I wonder if the pill is causing him pain.

"You okay?" I whisper. He nods and grunts, and I grab hold of his ass, pushing him into me with each thrust.

16

"Andreas, wait!"

We turn to Wulf, who holds out a DVD case. "Your first show—they're selling out as fast as we can burn them. Congratulations, you are officially Amsterdam's hottest sex act."

Andreas takes the DVD and shakes Wulf's hand. "Thanks, man. For everything—you've saved us, you really have."

Wulf claps him on the shoulder. "You're welcome. You've saved *me*, and this theater. Now go greet your fans."

My gaze darts to the door and the man standing there. Twice as dark—and big—as Andreas, I shoot him a smile. "Fans?" I ask.

"Ja. You're very popular." He winks.

"Watch it, man," Andreas warns.

The doorman raises his palms in capitulation and chuckles. "No offence, man, we good?"

Andreas nods. "How many are there?"

He peeks through the spyhole. "Couple of dozen at least."

"Don't worry, Kurt's the best, he'll make sure you get to your car in one piece," Wulf says.

I turn back to him and give him a small smile.

"Thanks again, man," Andreas says, shaking Wulf's hand once more. "See you Monday."

"Night, man."

"Night," I add, then turn back to Kurt and take a deep breath. He opens the door and we're hit by a barrage of camera flashes. *Damn cellphones!*

"Come on, lieveling," Andreas says, taking my elbow. "The sooner we face them, the sooner we get home."

I take another deep breath, hoping the creep from the last show isn't here, then plaster a smile on my face and step outside.

"Lola! Lola! Over here! Lola!"

"I love you, Lola!"

"Lola, you're gorgeous! Look over here!"

My smile becomes genuine as I soak up the compliments and admiration, and I step forward, pen in hand, to start signing DVD cases.

"Thank you, beautiful!"

"I'm gonna enjoy this!"

"Can't wait for the next show!"

"Stand back, give her room!" Kurt barks; he and Andreas working in tandem to push the throng of men back.

"She'll sign them all, stop crowding her," Andreas adds.

I glance up at him. He's not enjoying this; not one "fan" has shouted *his* stage name.

I keep signing, relishing the attention. In reaction to my smile, the men push forward again and I step back while Andreas and Kurt regain control.

Running my fingers through my hair, I fluff it and

shake my head to let it cascade down my back. I unbutton my coat and pose with my hand on my hip, now smiling genuinely for the camera phones.

I feel something brush my back and turn, but see nothing and nobody. The alley is dark, though only a few steps away from the stage door, and there's not much room. I shrug it off and turn back at an especially loud shout of "Lola, I love you". It was probably just a swirl of wind catching my coat.

It takes an hour to sign all the DVDs and make our way to the car, and I get in with a sigh and a giggle.

Andreas forces his frame into the tiny Mini and grimaces. I laugh. "Don't worry, we'll get a bigger car soon."

"Ja." He falls silent, unmoving, the keys still in his hand.

"What is it?" I ask, resting my hand on his thigh. "What's wrong?"

"Are you sure you're okay with all this? All this exposure and attention?"

"Yes," I say. "Yes, I am. When we're on that stage, I feel so alive. All those eyes watching me love you, watching us love each other. It really turns me on. It's like we—and our love—are the only things in the world."

"But all that, at the door, that's only going to get worse, you know."

"I hated it last night," I admit. "But tonight, I don't know, I relaxed and found it exciting. I felt safe with Kurt there as well."

"*Kurt* made you feel safe?"

"Well, yes, but only as backup for you," I mollified. "It just became an extension of the stage show; a fantasy, a titillation."

"But those men . . ."

"Those men are sad, lonely old fucks who can't get a—well—fuck. They're scared of real women and settle for fantasy and possibility rather than reality and real touch. They're harmless."

"But that creep last night?"

"Just got a bit carried away. It's okay. When we go out, we're always together. When we move into the new place, we'll have security. And at the theater, Kurt's there too."

"You seem to think a lot of Kurt."

I laugh. "Andreas, are you jealous? That's ridiculous, we just fucked—twice—on stage and in public. *You* are my man, always will be. I couldn't imagine doing that with anyone else. You have nothing to worry about."

"Don't I?"

"No! You don't! What's brought this on? You've never been insecure before."

"I just . . . worry."

"Worry?"

"Yes, worry. This is all a bit . . . extreme." He waves toward the theater. "It's so new and so . . . hardcore. And you're loving it. I worry about Pandora's box."

"Pandora's box?"

"Yes, you know, Pandora opens the box and lets all the evils out into the world. I'm wondering what we've let out of the box, and where it will lead."

"Andreas, honey." I turn and rest my other hand on his

chest, cursing the confines of the Mini. "It'll lead wherever we want it to lead, and if it goes somewhere either of us doesn't like, we stop. Simple as that."

"Is it?" He pushes the key into the ignition and the car stutters into life. "What if you *can't* stop?" He guns the engine and the car shoots off. I'm thrown back against the seat and by the time I recover myself, the moment for reassurance is gone.

17

"Drink?"

"Oh God, yes. Every muscle in my body hurts."

Andreas moves to the kitchen to fix the vodkas and I shrug my coat off, pausing as something falls out of the pocket. I hang up the coat, bend to pick up the piece of folded paper and stroll into the kitchen.

Andreas is waiting, finally with a smile on his face, although it looks forced. He holds out a half-liter glass of vodka and tonic. I laugh, cross over to him and take it.

I stretch up to him, one hand behind his neck and kiss him.

"You don't need to worry, Andreas, *nothing* is as important to me as you are."

He nods.

"Are *you* okay with what we're doing? I know it was your idea, but . . ."

"Shh, yes, I'm fine, it's just everything's turned around so well and so suddenly. There's usually a price to pay when that happens. I'm just concerned about how high that price will be."

I drop my hand from his neck and sip my drink. I have no idea what to say.

"Hey, Liesel." He strokes my cheek. "I'm sorry, don't

let me put a damper on everything, we'll be fine."

I look up at him. "Yes, we will. We've been through hell this past couple of years; first me losing my job, then you yours. We've suffered. This is our reward for getting through it—together."

He glances at the floor, then looks up at me. "Yes, I'm sure you're right. What's that?"

I furrow my brow, following his eyes to my hand. "Oh, I don't know. It fell out of my coat."

He takes it from me and opens it. He stares at it a while, then screws it up.

I put my drink down. "What? What is it?"

"Nothing. Just someone getting carried away again."

"Show me."

"It's nothing, Liesel."

"Show me!"

He hands it over and I smooth the paper out. It's a note, addressed to me.

Dear Liesel,

Please forgive my behavior the other night, it was unforgivable but you've just had such an impact on me.

Watching you on that stage, well, it was like an epiphany. I fell in love with you as soon as that bed turned around and wish, more than anything, that I could be a part of your life.

What are you doing with that black bastard? Oh sure, he has a dick on him, but you can do so much better. Look where he's brought you—onto a stage, exposing yourself, demeaning yourself, exploiting you.

If you were my wife, I'd give you everything you

desire, everything you deserve. You'd never have to suffer filthy eyes on you again. I'd treat you like a queen.

I love you,

"Oh my God, Andreas! It's him, that creep—he was there again tonight. He got close. Oh my God, he touched me." My eyes scan the note again and my heart misses a beat.

"Andreas, look. Look at the name." I thrust the note at him. "He knows my fucking name!"

Andreas grabs me in a fierce hug. "He probably just heard me asking if you were okay."

I nod. "But this—he must have written this in the theater, or even before. Shit, Andreas, I've got a stalker!"

"The sign of success."

I can feel his smile and pull away. "This isn't funny, it's serious! God knows what he's capable of. We have to call the police."

He pulls me close again. "He hasn't done anything and they won't take any action. They'll just call it fan mail."

"But . . ."

"Shh. We'll be careful. We'll keep an eye out and I'll have a word with Wulf and Kurt. Can you remember what he looked like?"

"Not really. Tall, dark hair, *respectable*." I gave a strangled laugh.

"Well, there you are then—respectable. Relax, you just have your first fan, that's all. We'll be careful, we're moving next week. You said yourself we're always together when we're out, and the new place is secure." His hug tightens and I relax a little. He's right.

He pulls back and smiles at me. "I love you, Liesel, I won't let anything happen to you."

I try to smile back; my nod is more successful.

"Now, take your drink." He passes me my glass and I take it, gulping the fizzy, fiery liquid. "It's been a long night, how about we go through and . . . watch a movie?" He waggles both the DVD and his eyebrows.

I laugh and relax. "Ooh, yes. That's a great idea."

I follow him into the sitting room and try to push away my feelings of unease.

18

I curl up next to Andreas and glance up at his profile as he presses "play". He smiles back and I look at the screen—for some reason embarrassed. I know the show felt good, but how had it looked? How had *I* looked, losing control as I came?

The opening titles come up:

Theater Voyeur

Oudezijds Achterburgwal
Amsterdam
Presents:

Darcy and Lola

The dark-red curtains swish open and the spotlight comes on, illuminating my back in my red robe. "Oh God, I was so scared," I whisper.

"I can't believe how brave you were—out there on your own."

"There was so much . . . feeling. Terror, excitement, I thought my heart was going to burst out of my chest."

"Here you come . . ."

I giggle and watch the bed revolve and my robe drop.

"Oh Liesel, my beautiful, sexy Liesel."

"I didn't realize quite how see-through that negligee was under those lights."

Andreas looks at me and bursts out laughing, missing his own entrance onto the stage.

I hit him with a pillow, but can't help joining in with his laughter.

"See-through," he splutters, incapable of more words.

"Shh, you're up."

"Oh, I want to see this bit."

I laugh and hit him with the cushion again. "Andreas, bloody hell, we've missed it—rewind!"

He hits the button then changes back to "play". We both stare at the screen as his hands stroke my body then pull apart my negligee, exposing me to the theater and camera.

"Oh God, that was so hot!"

"You're telling me." His hand caresses my thigh and I move to give him better access to my body. Feeling his hand on me as I watch him caress me is unbelievably exciting. I shift again.

"Strip," he says, his voice hoarse.

"You too," I reply, standing up and shedding my clothes as quickly as possible.

Back on the sofa, both naked, I spread my legs and he fingers me, keeping time with his hand on the screen.

"Ow, ow, Andreas, stop, I'm too sore." I'm nearly in tears.

He gives a soft laugh and says, "I'm not surprised! Lie down."

He moves, and I sprawl across the sofa, my gaze still fixed on the TV to watch the bed change position again. I catch my breath, knowing what's coming.

Andreas pushes my legs further apart—I hook one over the back of the sofa and brace the other against the floor. He kneels and nuzzles his face between my legs. I gasp—alternately looking at him and the TV.

I see myself notice the screen as Andreas licks my clit and I moan, my hips bucking of their own accord.

Simultaneously coming into Andreas' mouth and onto Andreas' cock, I yelp. I watch him fuck me doggy-style and his tongue feels as big and as hard as I remembered his cock to be.

I scream another orgasm and drench his face with my juice.

Panting, I lift his head. I can't take any more. "Stand up," I say, and sit up. I position him in front of me, but also so I can still see the TV.

I lick his balls, teasing my tongue around and between them before taking them into my mouth, one at a time, and gently sucking.

Andreas groans and I glance up to see him twist to watch the screen. I smile and lick the entire length of his cock, teasing the tip with my tongue and teeth.

Glancing back at the screen, I take him slowly into my mouth, but only slightly, and play with him some more. I want to get my timing right.

I watch myself approach orgasm and thrust my mouth down on him as I come again and again, then suck. The music grows louder and I remember he was about to come on stage.

I work my mouth hard—sucking and thrusting, and grab the root of his cock with my hand, immediately matching the rhythm of my mouth.

Andreas groans repeatedly and I suck hard, watching

him come as I feel the orgasm build up in him.

There: I both see and feel his back arch. Fighting a gag as he thrusts hard into my mouth, I squeeze slightly and get ready—unable to take my eyes off the stage.

He roars and spurts into my mouth, filling me. I swallow and accept more, then more. I grab his ass as I continue to move my mouth up and down, gently now.

Another roar, and another delicious mouthful. I swallow and withdraw, licking his shaft as I move.

I taste the last drops from his tip then look up at him and lick my lips.

"My God, Liesel, that was . . . that was . . ." He falls onto the sofa, unable to finish his sentence.

"Crazy," I finish for him, curling back up against him to watch the curtain close.

19

I grow sleepily aware of Andreas' arm circling me and his hand stroking my belly. I squirm backwards, nestling further into his embrace, and his hand moves to my breast. I make a small noise of approval in the back of my throat and his hand moves down my body to my groin.

I moan louder and his hand presses between my legs.

"Owa!" I'm suddenly wide awake, and not in a good way.

"You okay?"

"No. Shit, I'm sore!"

He withdraws his hand and gives a small laugh. "I'm not surprised!"

I turn to him and kiss him. "I'm sorry."

"Shut up, Liesel."

I smile back at him and kiss him more deeply. We linger, then he breaks away.

"Not fair, Liesel," he says with a grin, then pulls away and gets out of bed.

My face twists into a grimace. I might be sore, but I was enjoying that! I snuggle back into the pillow, pull the covers up around my shoulders and drift.

I wake again when Andreas sits on the bed. "Time to get up, sleepyhead, it's moving day, lots to do."

I try to pull the covers up over my head, but he grabs

them and yanks them down. I'm about to retaliate when I realize he's holding a mug of coffee. I take it and grin up at him. Then his words penetrate and I sit up, spilling coffee on the white bed linen.

"We're moving today."

He chuckles and stands. "You've got five minutes while I have a shower, then it's time to get up."

In answer, I blow my coffee and sip.

♥

I put plates filled with ham, cheese, eggs and toast onto the table and Andreas glances up at me. "Where are the rolls?"

I shake my head and finger the note from the last show which is in the pocket of my robe. I'd read it again once I'd got up and hadn't dared go to the bakers.

"Stop it, Liesel!"

I look up at him.

"I know it's got to you, but I won't let him hurt you."

"I think we should tell the police," I say again.

"And what will they do? Like I said last night, he hasn't done anything—they'll just dismiss it as fan mail and send us on our way."

"I suppose." I'm near tears and Andreas stands up and takes me into his arms.

"Shh, stop worrying. We're moving today, there's security at the theater, and I won't let you out of my sight—you're safe."

I nod against his chest, sniff and blink a few times, then push away. "Yes, you're right. I'm being silly, sorry. Would you like more coffee?"

He doesn't let go of me. "Sure? You're not just putting on a brave face?"

"No, I'm fine, honestly. Coffee?"

He stares at me a minute, then relaxes and nods. "Yes please." He sits and I pour us both a refill from the pot.

I join him at the table and the buzzer goes. "That'll be Wulf," Andreas says and jumps up to the intercom to release the front doors.

For a brief moment I consider berating him for not checking it *is* Wulf before unlocking, then I change my mind and shut my mouth. But I don't relax until Wulf enters.

"Morgen, any more coffee?"

Andreas pours him a cup and he joins us at the table then helps himself to breakfast. "All ready?" he asks, his mouth full of meat, and I wince at the sight.

"Yup, all packed. We can't wait to get out of this dump, eh, Liesel?"

I finally smile. "Yes. A new start. A new life." I sip my coffee as Andreas squeezes my hand.

"Right, we'd better get a move on." Wulf stands and drains his coffee. "I'm double- parked."

"Now you tell us! All we need is for your van to get clamped. If we're not out of here by tomorrow, the landlord will send his thugs around to throw us out."

"I'll go down and keep an eye on it. You two boys start humping boxes." I grin at Andreas, and Wulf winks at me. I force a smile at him and go downstairs.

♥

It doesn't take long to clear the apartment. Anything of value, except the TV, has long been sold. I don't go back up for a last look around. I'm done with that life.

"It's hardly inconspicuous," I whisper to Andreas.

Wulf's van has "Theater Voyeur" emblazoned on the side. "What if he's watching and follows us?"

"I know, but have you seen anyone hanging about, Liesel? 'Cause I haven't. It's fine, we'll be in the Mini and I'll keep an eye on the mirrors, make sure we're not followed."

I nod, then climb into the car and wait for Andreas to join me. He sets off and Wulf follows in the van. But I can't settle. I should be excited. Instead I stare out the windows, glaring at every man we pass.

"Andreas, that was him!"

"Where? Where?" He brakes, glances round, and bends to get a better view in the side mirror.

"We just passed him. He saw us, he was staring at the van. That guy in the hat."

"Are you sure it's him?"

"Yes. No. I think so."

♥

We pull up to the gates of our new house, and Wulf jumps out of his van almost before it comes to a stop. "What was that all about, Andreas? I nearly ran into the back of you."

Andreas sighs. "A guy who keeps hassling Liesel at the stage door. She thinks he's stalking us."

"What? Where?"

"Back there." Andreas gestures at the road.

"Does Kurt know?"

"Yes."

"Well, you'll be alright, he knows what he's doing. Anyway, you're wanted." He nods to the security guard.

Andreas moves to speak to him, and after a few

moments he opens up and lets us through.

"No one will get to you here, Liesel," Andreas says with a smile, squeezing my knee. As the gates clang shut behind us, I finally relax.

20

I look around me and grin. Our stuff doesn't even fill one room and we have no furniture to speak of, only a TV, DVD player and a camping table and chairs. I've just sent Andreas and Wulf out to buy a mattress. The bed will have to wait a week or two until we have time to go shopping.

I hug myself. I don't care that we have no furniture and very few belongings. We have a home.

The door bangs open and Wulf walks in backwards, followed by a plastic-wrapped mattress and Andreas. I point them upstairs to the bedroom Andreas and I have decided to make the master. The largest of the three choices, it looks over the Keizersgracht Canal with floor-to-ceiling windows and a door to our very own balcony.

While they bump their way upstairs, I rummage in our boxes to find bedding and follow them.

Andreas takes the box from me and I follow him into the room. Empty but for the mattress and with the ceiling soaring above us, it's beautiful—except for Wulf's presence, but he won't be staying much longer.

"Do you want a hand, lieveling?"

"No, I'm okay. You two go and get some wine and food while I make the bed, then we can chill."

"Sure?"

"Sure."

♥

An hour later they're back and I look up sharply—*what took them so long?*

"Sorry, lieveling," Andreas says with a glance at Wulf. I nod and relax, then hold out my hand for the bag of food.

While I plate up the Indonesian curry, Andreas opens a bottle of wine and finds some glasses—at least one of them is a wine glass—which he fills and passes to me.

We clink to our new home, and drink.

"Hey, what about me?"

Andreas grins at Wulf and hands him a glass of wine. "Thanks man, we'd have been stuck without you."

Wulf holds the glass up for another toast.

"That's all you're having, though, Wulf, you're driving."

He looks at me, disappointed, and I return his stare. There's no way he's staying over on our first night here.

I turn and pass him a plate, then give Andreas his and follow them back into the living room with my own hands full.

♥

Andreas takes the empty plates and nods at me to follow.

"Come on, Liesel, can he stay? We've got three bedrooms here and we wouldn't be here without him—in more ways than one."

"Andreas . . ."

"I know, it's not ideal, but it would mean a lot to him—and me."

He steps towards me and wraps his arms around my waist. I look into his eyes, curse the puppy-dog expression he's so good at, and shrug. "I guess he's not so bad, but only if he behaves!"

"'Course he will. Thanks, lieveling."

We go back to the sitting room to join our guest, Andreas carrying another bottle of wine.

I truly relax when I see Wulf has got out a pouch of tobacco and is busy rolling a joint.

"Where's the remote?" Andreas distracts me. I laugh.

"I've no idea, you'll have to use your finger!"

♥

Andreas gives me a kiss and leaves with Wulf to get more alcohol; the three bottles of wine hadn't lasted us two hours. I sit at the table to roll another joint.

Lighting it, I turn the music up and draw deep. My body moves to the music—Adele's *Make You Feel My Love*—of its own accord and I give into it.

I take a last drag on the joint, stub it out, and take to the floor again: swaying, moving every part of me to the melody, feeling it in every fiber of my being. My arms twist, my hands are in my hair, then travel down my body. My hips twitch to the beat, but it's not enough.

Slowly, I unbutton my shirt and shrug it off, do a slow twirl and see, through almost- closed eyes that Andreas and Wulf are standing in the doorway. I don't miss a beat, but feel a smile spread my lips.

I slowly stroke my hands over my bra and belly, then move to my back and unzip my skirt. It falls and I step out of it, still keeping time to the music.

I dance around in a circle then, with my back to the

boys. I unclasp my bra, slide it down my arms, then hold it to one side, keeping the pose a moment before dropping it.

My hands caress my buttocks then move to my front, rising to my breasts before I turn. I bring them up to my shoulders, then push my fingers into my hair and arch my back, my feet still moving to the rhythm. I slide my hands back down my sides to my thong and I smile when I remember it's only held up by ribbons tied in bows.

I take hold of the ties and pull, opening my eyes to smile at Andreas as the scrap of lace and satin falls.

He pulls his t-shirt over his head and walks towards me. "Roll another joint, Wulf," he says. "Make it a strong one."

I don't look at Wulf—he's already seen everything I have to offer in intimate detail, magnified God knows how many times on that stage LED screen.

Andreas rests his hands on my hips and sways to the rhythm. I grasp his belt, unfastening it in one motion then, hungry now, I unsnap the buttons of his jeans and push them down.

While he struggles out of them, I stretch my arms over my head, my hands clasped, and I continue to dance; aware of Wulf staring.

I cross over to him, bend, take the joint from his fingers and savor the smoke filling my lungs before blowing it into his face.

I sashay back to Andreas, wriggling my ass for Wulf's benefit, take another drag and pass the joint to my husband.

As he takes his own draw, I dance around him, caressing his body, and close my hand around his cock.

But I want to tease so I don't stroke, but run my fingers up and down his shaft before tickling his balls. He groans a lungful of sweet smoke into my face and I breathe deeply.

He grasps my ass with one hand and kneads, then runs a finger up the middle to the small of my back.

I giggle and nip his chest with my teeth, then take back the joint so he has both hands free.

He uses his newly unencumbered hand to cup my breast and guides my nipple into his mouth. I throw my head back as sensations course through me—straight to my vagina. I move my legs apart and Andreas responds, moving his other hand around to my groin and sliding his finger between my lips.

"Oh God, Liesel, you're so wet!"

In answer I tilt my hips forward, splaying my knees slightly, and he slips his finger inside me. I groan and throw my head back, forcing my nipple further between his teeth and deepening the penetration of his finger. He moves it in circles and tickles the walls of my vagina, and I cry out my first orgasm. I remember my own free hand and take a tighter hold of his cock, pumping it up and down as he suckles and finger-fucks me.

The joint is plucked from my fingers and I dig my nails into Andreas' back, feeling another hand stroke my back down to my ass. Wulf caresses my buttocks then pushes his hand between my legs, tickling my sphincter.

I moan. *Shit, I'm stoned!* As he pushes in, Andreas

becomes aware of his penetration and shouts.

Suddenly I'm bereft of touch and am pushed to the side as Andreas grabs Wulf—whom I now realize is also naked.

I move back to the table out of the way as they fight, and pour myself a drink. They're both on the floor and my hand creeps to my clit as I watch the show.

Andreas finally lands a fist somewhere painful and Wulf rolls away. Andreas gets to his feet and grabs the pile of Wulf's clothes, then marches to the front door, throws them outside, and comes back for Wulf.

"Sorry, sorry, mate, I got carried away. No offense."

"No offense? You put hands on my wife!"

"I know, I know, too much to drink and smoke and what you were doing—it was too much for me. Sorry, mate."

"Get the fuck out." Andreas sounds weary now. "Just get out."

Wulf circles Andreas, then bolts for the door, limp dick bobbing pathetically, and I collapse into giggles.

Andreas slams the door, glares at it, then comes back into the room, still looking angry, but I can't stop laughing and fall off my chair.

"Bloody hell, Liesel, this is getting out of hand."

"He-he-he-he tried-tried . . ." Coherent words can't find their way past my giggles. I give up and surrender to the laughter.

"You're drunk, stoned, whatever. How much weed did you smoke while we were gone? Never mind." He despairs of getting an answer. "Time for bed."

He bends, picks me up and carries me upstairs. I reach for his cock and he shifts my position in his arms so I can't grab it.

"No, I've had enough for one night."

He dumps me on the bed, gets me under the covers and goes back downstairs.

I know I should follow him, but suddenly I'm too tired. I close my eyes and am asleep in moments.

21

Andreas takes my coat and I smile up at him, then peer into the dressing room mirror. Things have been strained, to say the least, all day and we haven't talked properly yet. *How on earth are we supposed to have sex on stage to entertain, when he can barely look at me?*

"I'm so sorry, Andreas," I say, yet again. He grunts.

"Andreas." He turns to look at me, eyebrows raised.

"Please, we need to talk or we're not going to be able to do this."

"The show? That's what you're worrying about? Letting down your adoring men?"

"No!" I shout, then pause, take a breath and run my fingers through my hair. "Not the show: us. If this—" I wave my hands around to indicate the theater "—will break us, I don't want to do it. I'd rather be penniless and on the street."

He stares at me, but says nothing.

"I mean it. It was supposed to be fun, exciting. And it was supposed to be about us."

"It wasn't just about us last night."

"Yes it was! I just got wasted and horny, and Wulf took it too far. I didn't invite him."

"You stripped for him. Danced naked in front of him."

"I stripped and danced for *you*! I didn't think anything of him—he was just our audience. He sees me naked four times a week."

"Only on stage, not at home."

"And in here," I remind him. "He's your friend, I *never* thought he'd try to join in!"

Andreas relaxes and I step toward him. "I love you, I love making love to you, and I love having people watch. But if it's too much, we'll stop, keep it private again."

He grins wryly. "That wouldn't be enough for you— not anymore."

"*You're* enough for me—that's all that matters." I put my arms around him and kiss his unresponsive lips. "Just say the word and we'll walk away from this— now." I kiss him again; this time he responds.

"Okay?" I ask.

He kisses me again and says, "Okay." My heart sinks a little, despite what I said. I don't want to stop the shows. "But we need to keep the exhibitionism in the theater and not bring it home. Deal?"

I relax. "Deal."

He kisses me harder and unzips my dress, then pushes it from my shoulders. I step out of it and stop as the door opens.

Wulf sticks his head in and immediately flushes red. "Fifteen minutes," he mumbles and backs out, letting the door slam shut.

I look at Andreas and give a nervous laugh. "You need to talk to him, clear the air—we have to work with him, after all."

"I know. But not tonight. Let him stew a few days first."

"Andreas, I never realized you were so mean."

He shrugs. "Only to friends who betray me."

I quieten and watch him, then sigh with relief when he smiles and pulls his shirt off. "Come on, get the rest of your clothes off—we've got fifteen minutes to get oiled up and do our makeup."

♥

I lie on my back in the dark, naked. My arms are stretched up beyond my head. Black silk to match the black satin sheets ties one wrist, is fastened round a shackle attached to the base of the bed and facing the auditorium, then binds my other wrist. I'm spread-eagled across the sheets and have never felt so vulnerable.

I hear the swish of the curtains and the creak of the pulleys from the ropes controlling them, and gasp as a single spotlight glares into life, focused on my body. I look up at the huge mirror suspended above the stage and blink in the reflected glare. I can't see the people out there, but they can see every bit of me.

The theater is full: Word has got around and we're popular. I have no idea if anyone I know is out there. I turn my head at a touch to my cheek, kissing the lips that press to mine.

"Alright, lieveling?" Andreas asks.

I smile. I'm not alright, not really, but I'd agreed to be tied up like this and it's too late to back out now. Anyway, I know I'll enjoy it when we get going.

His hand strokes my jawline, then my throat. It moves lower, cupping my left breast, then kneads me before circling and tweaking my nipples. His mouth and tongue take over and his hand is free to travel lower.

Fingers skim the side of my belly, then trace the join of my leg to my hip—inner to outer—and I groan. I want his hand to move in the other direction.

He strokes my hip, crosses my knee, and caresses my inner thigh—moving slowly, ever so slowly, but getting closer.

Finally he reaches the center of me; first stroking, then circling around my clit. I lift my hips, wanting more pressure, and moan—a sound that is echoed by I don't know how many throats.

I glance up at the mirror—I can't see the screen from here without moving and spoiling the view for the punters—trying to see what they see. I part my legs a little wider and lift my pelvis towards the camera.

"See, I knew you'd love it," Andreas whispers in my ear. I turn to him and kiss him.

He's right. I feel alive, daring, beautiful, loved—and I want to share that love with anybody who wants to watch.

Andreas is everything to me. I hated the past day of us fighting. I love him so much and can't get enough of him: his mouth, his body, his cock. And if people want to pay to watch us love—where's the harm?

He moves his hand, pulling my thigh toward him. I shift on the bed so that we're almost at right angles; my left leg between his, my right held up in the air.

I jerk my hands, wanting to reach between my legs to hold him, stroke him, but the bindings don't give. I arch my back and neck in frustration and he plunges into me.

I gasp. He hasn't held back and I lift my pelvis to open as wide as I can to him.

I meet his eyes and he smiles, withdraws, and thrusts into me again. I gasp and glance up at the mirror, wondering if they can all see every detail of our penetration. *Yes, they can.*

Again, again, again he slams into me and I scream my first orgasm—putting the vocals on a bit for the audience, I admit, but I can't fake the spasms shuddering through my body.

I'm shocked to have come so hard and so soon, and I glance up at him. He smiles and shoves his full length inside me again. I gasp and realize he's taken one of the blue pills. I wonder for a moment if I'm going to be able to keep up.

His hand lets go of my right leg and he circles my clit again. I groan and jerk against my bonds; this is almost too much.

But not quite. My pelvis lifts in another orgasm, and I feel a deep heat explode within me. Then again, and again, and again. I cry out—no theatrics this time, this is all real—and come again, even louder.

I slump back on the sheets, trying to get my breath, but Andreas doesn't pause. I shift slightly, and he reaches even further inside me—hitting that spot. I writhe on the bed, not noticing I'm rubbing my wrists sore on their ties.

The next orgasm builds deep inside and from my clitoris at the same time. I give myself to it utterly; completely unaware now of where I am. More ejaculate spews over Andreas and the satin sheets, but I can't stop coming and he doesn't still his fingers or his cock.

Again, again, again. I feel faint now and want it to stop, but my mouth can't form the words. He grunts and I feel his cock spasm inside me—it makes my next orgasm even more intense and we come together over and over.

Our bodies calm and we smile at each other, then

there's another grunt—he's come again, and the feel of his orgasm is enough to trigger another in me. Finally, they stop and we relax onto the bed. I try to stroke his cheek and am surprised to find my hands bound—I'd forgotten.

The light douses and I hear the swish and creak of the curtain closing despite the music.

I still can't move. Andreas reaches under the bed for our robes and Wulf rushes onto stage with scissors. Andreas snatches them off him and cuts me free. I kneel on the bed, massage my wrists, and give Wulf an embarrassed smile.

He stands, frozen, staring at me until Andreas puts the robe over my shoulders and whispers in my ear, "Show's over, Liesel, stop teasing him."

I twist my neck to kiss him and his hand caresses my breast once more.

"That's enough, you two. Get off the stage, the next act's ready."

We break apart and grin at Detlef. Wulf has already scurried away. I slide my arms into my robe, belt it and gingerly climb off the bed.

22

Kurt opens the stage door for me and I smile my gratitude. His return gaze is stony, and my heart sinks. *What's Wulf been saying? Does everyone know?* We hadn't seen him since he brought the scissors on stage, and I glance up at Andreas when he taps my ass—I suppose for reassurance.

A deep breath, then I'm through the door, a smile plastered on my face. Cell flashes blind me, but I keep going, sign DVD cases and even one man's chest. I move up the line, knowing Andreas and Kurt are right behind me, then my arm is grabbed and I'm pulled hard.

I stumble and move with the man to keep my footing, scream and look at him. It's the creep from the first night.

"Andreas!" *Where is he?*

I glance behind to see the other men surrounding both Andreas and Kurt—they can't break free, I'm on my own.

I try to wrench my arm free, but he's strong—my bicep feels as if it's gripped by a gigantic pair of pliers. I have no choice but to stumble along with the man.

"Liesel!" Finally, Andreas is coming. I scream his name and suddenly he's there.

My arm is freed and I scurry away. "Andreas!" He's

not coming with me, but lunges at my abductor. Then Kurt is here too and rushes at the two struggling men.

It's dark and I can't see well. I look around and realize we're in one of the alleys behind the theater, then I scrabble around in my bag for my phone.

"Run, Liesel, run!" Andreas shouts, and I look up in alarm as his final word becomes a scream.

At the panic in his voice, I obey and run—stumbling along through my sobs.

I trip and scream as a strong arm breaks my fall. "It's okay, Liesel, come on, keep going."

I sob in relief at the sound of Kurt's voice and allow him to pull me along. "Andreas?" I ask, my breath coming in gasps.

"He's hurt, that man had a knife."

"*What*? No! Andreas!" I stop and turn to go back to him.

"No!" Kurt bends and lifts me. I shriek for him to put me down.

"Wulf's with him, he'll be okay. He told me to get you somewhere safe. Wulf will call when it's okay."

I calm down and let Kurt carry me away, but stare over his shoulder into the black alleyway, desperate for Andreas.

"That creep's still out there, Liesel. I promised Andreas I'd look after you."

I drop my head and bury my face in his shoulder.

"It's okay, you can put me down, I'll walk."

"We're nearly there, Liesel. Trust me."

23

The bedroom feels wrong somehow, and I try to open my eyes. They don't move. *Am I even awake?* I slip back further into sleep and re-join my dream. Running. Being chased. I scream and am back in my bedroom. But it isn't my bedroom—I'm still dreaming. *Andreas— where's Andreas?* Something's happened. *What?*

I hear the door open and footsteps creak across the wood floor. *Wood floor?* We don't have a wood floor. Then I remember we moved. *Does the new house have wood floors?* I can't remember.

A clunk as something is put down on the bedside table and the mattress sinks as someone sits down. *Andreas? But why doesn't he say anything? Am I still dreaming?*

A hand strokes my face, pushing my hair away from my eyes and mouth. A tender hand; a loving hand.

"Liesel?"

My breath catches and I panic. I'm definitely awake. But that isn't Andreas' voice, and I can't move. *Why can't I move?*

The man shakes my shoulder and my paralysis breaks. My eyes open and I blink. I try to scrabble backwards, but the man takes a firm grip of the shoulder he's just gently shaken.

"Liesel, it's okay. Wake up, it's me, Kurt."

"Kurt?"

"Yes."

"What am I doing here?"

"Don't you remember?"

I shake my head but flashes of my dream come back. Darkness, running, screaming, Kurt picking me up. Suddenly I remember. "Andreas! Where's Andreas? Is he okay?"

"Liesel, I'm sorry. Wulf has just called. That man who grabbed you . . ."

"He had a knife! He stabbed Andreas!" I sat up, the covers dropping from me. In the corner of my mind, I realize I'm naked, but don't care. "Where's Andreas? Kurt! Answer me—how is he?"

Kurt holds my other shoulder, his hands caressing me—moving down my arms, then back to my shoulders. He cups my neck and bends his head to touch his forehead to mine.

"Liesel, I'm so sorry," he whispers.

"No, no, no, no . . ."

"Andreas died, Liesel. Wulf did his best, but they couldn't save him."

"Nooo!" I wail, and Kurt embraces me, pulling me close to him and holding me tight, rocking me like a distraught child.

"I'm so sorry, Liesel. I'm so sorry. I didn't get there in time."

I try to pull away, but he won't let me. "Let me go, I need to see him."

"Liesel, no. I promised him I'd keep you safe and that's what I'll do. The police came earlier, but you were asleep. They said to stay here until they come back."

"But Andreas, he's all alone . . ."

"Shh, there's nothing you can do. I'll take you to see him when that bastard is caught. Now drink this. You've had a shock, it'll be good for your nerves."

I take the glass and sip, shake my head and try to give him back the glass. It's brandy. I don't want alcohol, I want to find Andreas.

Kurt pushes the glass back to my mouth and, with his other hand, holds the back of my head. He forces me to drink.

I splutter.

"All of it, Liesel." His grip is hard and I drink. I have no choice.

"There, that's better. Everything will be okay."

Okay? How will anything ever be okay again?

My eyelids feel heavy and droop closed against my will. Kurt gently lies me back down, pulling the covers over me.

I try to speak, but can't and I feel myself drift. *He's drugged me,* I think, *he's drugging me. Why?*

I can't form the words and even my thoughts are hazy now. I drift into darkness.

24

"Umm." I snuggle under the covers as Andreas caresses my body. His hand gently cups my breast and his thumb flicks my nipple. I wriggle under his touch, desire flooding my body.

My lips part as they meet his and his tongue flicks inside my mouth. I kiss him hungrily and a jolt of excitement makes my hips buck.

His hand slides down my body to between my thighs. They part of their own accord and he slides his finger along my cleft. I moan when he reaches my clit and circles it. My hips buck again and his finger slides into my vagina, tickling my G-spot. He slides out again, bringing more moisture with him and circles, teases and presses my clit. I moan as heat gathers in the tops of my legs and belly, and I thrust my hips to his hand.

He moves on top of me and the tip of his cock presses against the opening of my vagina. I thrust again, wanting him inside me. He grabs his cock and rubs it against my clit, then pushes into me as I come again. The sensation is overwhelming and my orgasm rebuilds until I'm coming over and over again.

"Liesel," he whispers and I still. I try to open my eyes, but my lids are too heavy.

I forget my disquiet as he bends his head to my breast

and suckles. His rhythm is so gentle, so tender, yet so filling; my body is lost in the ecstasy of his touch.

Another orgasm builds and I thrust my hips in time with his. Still building, still growing; then I cry out with the ferocity of my explosion.

He calls my name again and now my eyes open. I look up into his eyes.

"What . . .?"

"Shh, Liesel, it's okay. I love you. Everything's okay," Kurt says.

"No, no." I try to push him away, but he thrusts harder and my body responds, betraying me.

I moan, partly in pleasure, partly at the memories that flood me. Andreas. The creep. Alleys. Kurt. *Andreas is dead!*

Kurt's thrusts grow harder, and he rears up, gripping my buttocks and pulling me onto him as he pushes into me.

"No," I cry as another orgasm rips through me.

"That's it, Liesel, I know you want me. Come on, Liesel."

I want to get away but my body doesn't respond—not to me, anyway. Kurt's pounding increases—faster and even deeper—and he hits that spot deep inside me: Andreas' spot. I scream in pleasure and frustration. Kurt doesn't falter and I come again and again, until my juices gush from me.

He roars in approval and his own orgasm bursts into me.

He looks down at me, smiles, releases my ass and moves over me again to kiss me.

Finally my body is my own and I don't return his kiss.

It doesn't seem to bother him, and I let my mind drift back over the last few days.

I realize Kurt has kept me here drugged, but have no idea how long for. I remember he said the police would be coming, but now recognize that as a lie.

Kurt finally stops and rests his head beside mine, his body a dead weight on top of me.

Andreas—poor, poor Andreas. Has Kurt killed him? I remember the letter from my stalker—signed by 'R'. *No, not 'R'—'K'.* It was Kurt all along. The man hired to protect us killed Andreas—*what's he going to do with me? How long will he keep me here?*

25

I can barely breathe, and try to wriggle to the side. I manage about three inches, but at least I break the connection at our groins and he falls out of me.

Pausing for a minute, I realize my body still isn't right and wonder what drugs are still in my system.

I take a deep breath and push and slide again. Kurt groans and I whisper, "Hush, baby, it's okay."

He settles back into sleep and moves to the side. Now only my leg is trapped and I slowly pull it out, disgusted at the feel of him on my skin.

Finally I'm free and stand, then grab the bedside table as my legs threaten to buckle.

Kurt groans again and lifts his head. I grab the lamp and hit him. He roars in pain and reaches for me. Panicking, I hit him again and again until he's still.

Out of breath, I sit on the bed for a moment to gather my strength then harness my still- shaking legs and stagger to the door.

The hallway is dingy and dark, but a light shines at one end and I move toward it to find the front door.

Daylight shines through the small window in the door and I wrench at the handle, but the door doesn't budge.

Tears overwhelm me—*I'm so close*—and I rest my head against the door. Opening my eyes I see I'm still naked and know I need to go back to the bedroom.

My head is clearing a little and my legs feel stronger as I make my way back down the hallway.

Entering the room, I stare at the bed. Kurt is still out cold. *Have I killed him?* I shrug and hope I have—he killed Andreas.

His clothes are in a heap on the floor. I rummage in his jeans pocket and almost yell out loud when I find his keys.

Kurt groans at the noise and I freeze, staring at him.

His movements still and I let out my held breath. I briefly think about hitting him again, then turn and grab his overcoat from where it's hanging on the back of the door.

26

Hurrying along the hallway, I stumble and cry out as my ankle turns under me and I hit the floor. I stay where I am, not daring to move, and listen. Nothing.

I start breathing again and get to my feet, crying out again when I put weight on my ankle. I bend and massage it. It's tender, but I don't think it's broken. Even if it is, I still have to walk.

I shrug on the coat and button it up, then limp to the door, catching my breath as the key turns, but I don't relax until I'm outside with the door locked behind me. I tighten the belt of the coat and look around me, trying to work out where I am.

I can see a canal, but it's too small to be one of the ring canals. I don't recognize the street. I must be in the outskirts, but at least I'm still in Amsterdam.

A blue-and-white tram rumbles over a bridge and I limp toward the street it's driving down. I spot a stop close by and wait for the next one.

Two minutes later, a tram arrives and all its doors open. I move to the back and glance at the ticket counter. It's manned by a woman and I stay on the street.

Nervously, I wait for the next one, praying for a male conductor. I glance back up the street—no sign of Kurt, but he won't stay unconscious forever.

My heart jumps at the familiar rumble of another tram and relief floods through me to see a man sitting at the ticket counter—him I can handle. I let the other passengers get on first to make sure I'm last.

He looks up at me. "Please help me—I need to get to Oudekerk." I name the red-light district where the theater is situated.

"€2.80."

"I'm sorry, I don't have any money—I was mugged. They even took my clothes." I indicate my coat. "Please help me."

He raises his eyebrows, then looks me up and down. Now I relax and untie my belt, unfasten every button, and finally open my coat to his gaze.

He stares and licks his lips. The passengers protest at the delay and he glances around at them in annoyance, looks me up and down again, and nods for me to sit down.

I ignore the stares, male sniggers and female mutters, and find a seat. An old woman sits next to me and I prepare myself for a lecture. She puts a hand on my knee and peers into my face.

"Are you alright, dear?"

Her kindness floods my eyes with tears, but I can't break down now. I manage a small smile and nod, staring out the window.

After five minutes, I recognize the Oude Kerk—the old church—and get off a couple of stops later—fending off a couple of groping hands as I walk to the door.

Theater Voyeur is just around the corner and I hurry as well as I'm able in bare feet and with a sprained ankle.

27

"Oh my God, Liesel! Where have you been? Are you alright?" Wulf grabs me in a bear hug as soon as I walk through the stage door. "Christ, half the police in Amsterdam are out looking for you! Andreas is going out of his mind."

I pull away. "Andreas? He's alive? Oh Christ." I sink to the floor.

Wulf bends down and lifts me back to my feet. "Yes, yes, my God, you thought he was dead?"

"Where is he?"

"OLVG Hospital."

"Let's go."

"But the police . . ."

"Ring them when we get there, just get me to Andreas!"

"Okay, okay. Do you want to get changed first?"

"No! I want Andreas!"

"The van's just out back, come on then."

"You'll have to help me." I put my arm around his shoulders and brace myself against him, managing to keep most of my weight off my ankle.

"What is it? What's wrong?"

"It's just a sprained ankle, don't worry, just get me to the van."

"What happened, who did this to you?"

"Kurt."

"*Kurt?*"

"Yes." I didn't want to talk about it, not to Wulf.

He helps me into the van, then hurries around to the driver's door and gets in.

"How is he? Andreas?"

Wulf hesitates before answering. "He'll be okay, but he doesn't look good, Liesel, you need to prepare yourself."

"How badly was he hurt?"

"Well, the creep—no, Kurt—stabbed him. He was in surgery for hours. They took his spleen out, but managed to mend everything else. He won't be doing any shows for a while, but he'll be okay."

I nod. *Shit, how close did I come to losing him?* I don't want to ask.

"Let me call him," Wulf says.

"No! No, not over the phone, we'll be there in a few minutes. This is a face-to-face conversation."

"The police, then."

"Not till I've seen Andreas! They'll want to talk to me for hours—I need to see Andreas first."

"But Kurt—he'll get away!"

"He's not going anywhere—for a while at least."

Wulf glances at me, obviously curious, but stays silent as he drives.

28

Five minutes later, we're there. Wulf insists I get into a wheelchair as it'll be faster than limping and I agree. I get a lot of strange stares—I can't stop the coat falling open, exposing my bare legs, but I don't care; I just want to get to Andreas.

"Nearly there," Wulf says as the elevator doors open. "He's just down here." He greets the nurses behind the desk. "I've found her," he says. "Is he awake?"

They beam at me. "Yes, go through. This is just what he needs."

Wulf pushes me into a room and pulls the curtains open around a bed.

"Andreas," I whisper and get out of the wheelchair, then hobble to his bed, sit down and take his hand. My breath catches in my throat as I see how ill he looks.

"Andreas," I say, louder, and he opens his eyes.

"Liesel?" he croaks. "Is that really you?"

"Yes, lieveling, I'm here, how are you?"

"Never mind me, how are *you*? What happened? Where have you been?"

"I'm fine. Kurt took me—he was the stalker, even that note was from him. It was a 'K' not an 'R', it was him all along."

"Kurt? That bastard!" He tries to rise from the bed,

then winces and groans. I push him back down.

"Relax, lieveling, I'm okay, I got away."

"What did he do to you?"

I bite my lip and look down.

"Liesel?"

I glance back up at him. I have to tell him or he will never let it rest. "He . . . he told me you were dead."

"Dead? You thought I was dead?"

I nod. "He drugged me—I don't know how long for."

"It's been four days," Wulf says from the door.

"Four days!" I'm shocked.

"What else did he do, Liesel?"

I look back at Andreas. "He-he tried to have sex with me."

"Tried?"

I nod again. I can't tell him how far it went. "I hit him over the head with the table lamp and locked him in."

Andreas laughs, then grimaces. "Oh, don't make me laugh, it hurts!"

"Sorry, sorry! How badly are you hurt?"

"I'm okay." His eyes dart to the side and I know he's lying.

"Andreas?"

He pushes the covers down to show me the dressing that covers most of the left-hand side of his torso.

"Oh, Andreas!"

"It looks worse than it is. They've patched me up pretty good."

I swing my legs up and kneel on the bed to kiss him. "I'm so sorry, Andreas."

He pulls away. "Sorry?"

"Yes, I was so worried about that creep, I didn't spot it

was Kurt who was the threat."

He pushes my hair off my face. "Neither did I, Liesel. All that worry, and it was the security guard."

I laugh through tears, although none of this is funny. He can never know I fucked Kurt and enjoyed it—even though I'd thought it was Andreas making love to me.

"What's under that coat?"

I smile, kneel astride him, undo my belt and buttons and shrug it off—pushing memories of the tram ticket collector out of my mind.

Andreas frowns and I shake my head, then he relaxes, trusting me. "Leave us, Wulf. Guard the door."

"No problem." He sounds a bit put out, but I ignore him. I'm with Andreas. I've had enough of other men and being desired by them—for the moment.

The door closes and Andreas smiles up at me. "Now, where were we?"

I bend to kiss him and his hands feel so good on my body—the only hands that belong there.

I reach behind him to undo his gown and he does his best to help me, but can I tell every movement is hurting him. I resort to fisting the material in my hands and ripping the ties off. I throw the cotton to the floor and stare at his body, doing my best to ignore his dressings. I had thought him lost to me forever, I'm so moved to be touching him again and feeling him respond to me.

I kiss him once more, all the emotion of the last few days flooding out of me, and position myself over him. His hand guides himself and I slowly push down onto his cock, then rise and push down again.

"Oh, Liesel, I was so scared I'd never see you again."

"Me too," I whisper and speed up.

"Careful!" he squeals.

"Sorry." I slow my pace but go deep, shudders wracking my body.

He digs his fingers into my thighs and I lean forward and risk speeding up again.

"Is that okay?"

"Oh God, yes."

I brace my hands either side of his head and rock my hips, determined to lose all my senses except the sense of him; forcing the image and memory of Kurt's touch away.

Faster and harder, we're both crying out with every thrust, unable to help ourselves. I scream louder as Kurt's face swims in front of my eyes with another orgasm.

"What the hell's going on in here?"

Neither of us pauses at the woman's voice.

"Mr. Aalders?"

I can't stop. Neither of us can stop. I ram myself onto Andreas, determined to lose the memory of that other man, and can feel my orgasm build. Again and again until we both explode.

I collapse onto my husband, but he cries out in pain and I push myself up, then turn.

A shocked nurse and a police officer are in the doorway. An embarrassed Wulf pokes his head around them and apologizes. "I tried to stop them coming in, but they ignored me."

I smile and nod, lift myself off Andreas, retrieve my coat and pull the blanket up over Andreas. The nurse bustles over to check on him.

"Mrs. Liesel Aalders?" the police officer asks.

"Yes."

"Good to see you're alive and well."

Epilogue

Andreas is home. Kurt has been found; still unconscious but alive and is now in Bijlmerbajes prison awaiting trial. The police have finally finished with me; they debated about charging me for having sex with Andreas in the hospital room, but decided against it.

I curl up in the bed next to my husband and trail my fingers over his scar, thinking about how close we came to losing each other.

His hand moves to my breast and I reach over to switch out the light.

His touch becomes more insistent and his hand moves between my legs. I grasp his cock and stroke it, keeping pace with the rhythm of his fingers. As he grows more urgent, I match him, and his cock expands to its fullest in my grip. I stroke up and down, running my thumb around his tip, spreading the moisture there, then stroke again before cupping and massaging his balls.

He rolls on top of me and I lift and spread my knees. He pushes inside and I moan his name. He's feeling tender—or maybe just sore—and pushes slowly. I can feel every millimeter of him move against my vagina walls and tilt my hips to encourage him to push deeper.

My hips meet every thrust, my hands grip his ass and heat floods my body, but I can't look at him—even in the dark.

My head is turned away, even as I come, and I stare into the dark.

I'm safe, Andreas is healing, and we're together again. But I'm different. Kurt made me different, and I know life will never be the same again.

Liesel and Andreas' story continues in *Theater Voyeur Book 2—Camera,* coming soon

Reviews

Thank you for buying and reading *Theater Voyeur: Lights*. If you enjoyed it, please consider leaving a rating and review on Amazon and Goodreads. All genuine comments and feedback are extremely important to Annelise Fox and are very welcome.

Thank you.

About the Author

Annelise Fox was born in the Netherlands, and though she currently resides in the UK, her heart is still in Amsterdam.

Theater Voyeur: Lights is her first book, allowing her to give full rein to her darker side!

Book Two—*Camera*, and Book Three—*Action* will follow soon.